see you later alligator...

belongs to

Pat Mintun
360 Larita Drive
Ben Lomond, CA 95005

see you later alligator...

by Barbara Strauss and Helen Friedland

Illustrated by Tershia d'Elgin

PRICE/STERN/SLOAN
Publishers, Inc., Los Angeles
1987

This book is dedicated to Morgan,
Sara Lily, Jared and Megan.

SECOND PRINTING — MARCH 1987

See you in a towel, Owl.

See you at the show, Crow.

See you in a caboose, Moose.

See you in pajamas, Llamas.

See you eating honey, Bunny.

See you with a balloon, Raccoon.

See you at the lab, Crab.

See you at four, Dinosaur.

See you getting peppered, Leopard.

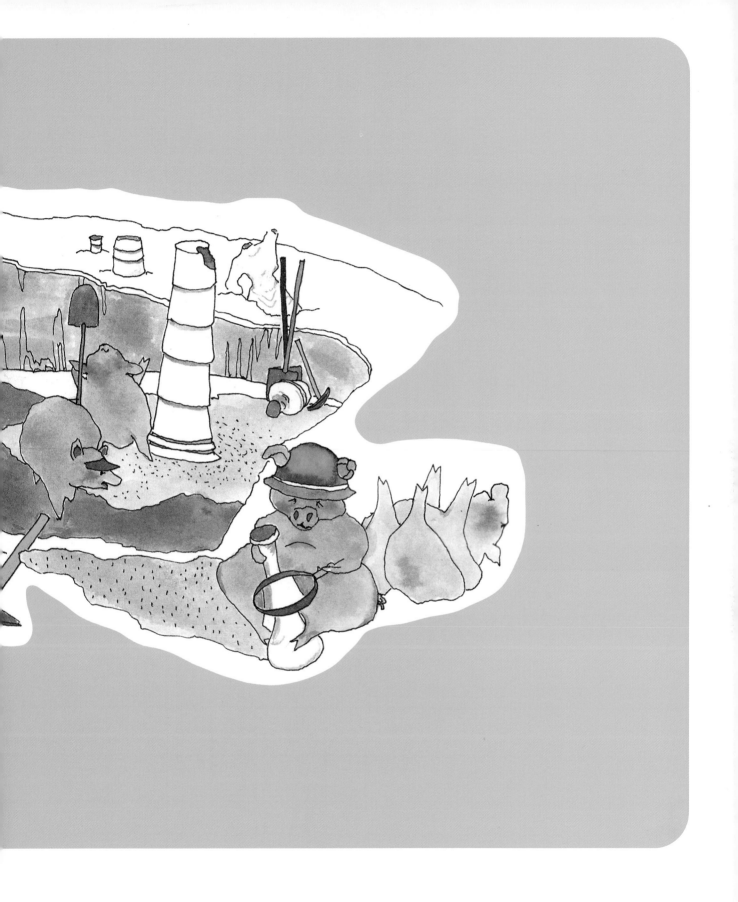

See you at the digs, Pigs.

See you in socks, Fox.

See you on the bus, Platypus.

See you for laughs, Giraffes.

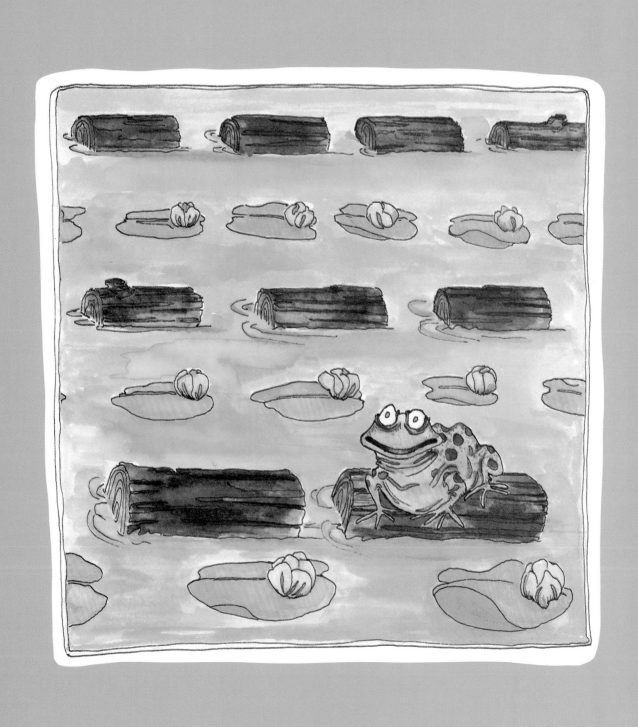

See you on the log, Frog.

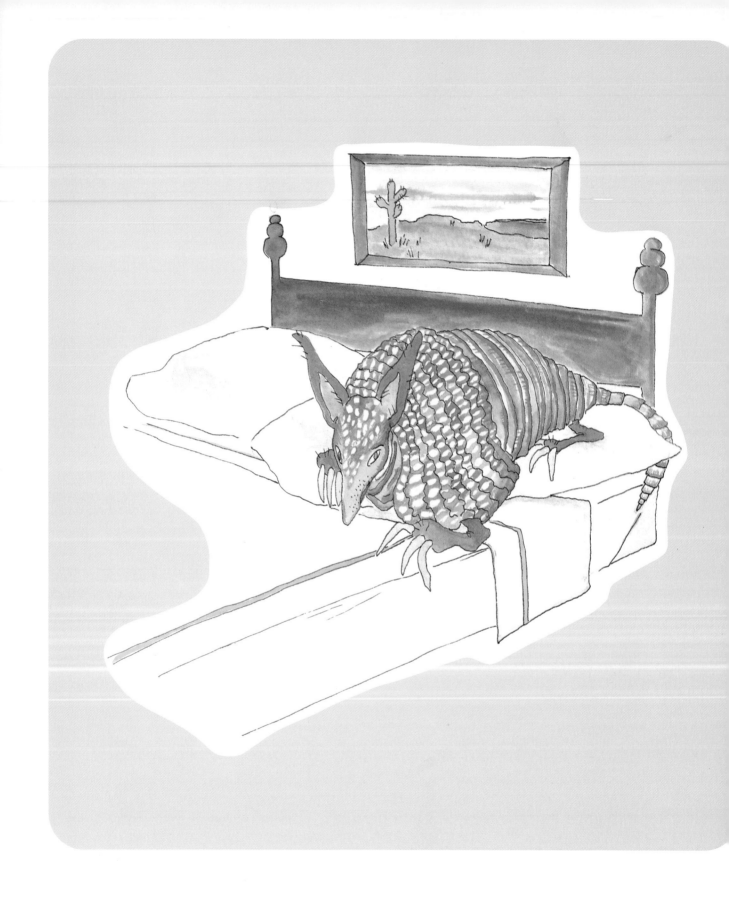

See you on my pillow, Armadillo.

See you at bat, Cat.

See you reading a paper, Tapir.

See you on skis, Fleas.

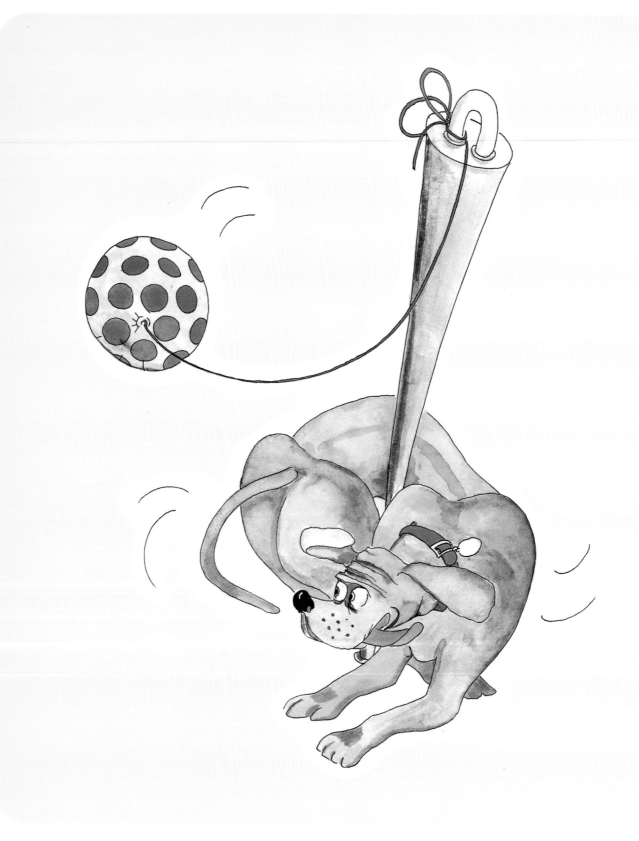

See you around, Hound.

See you on the veranda, Panda.

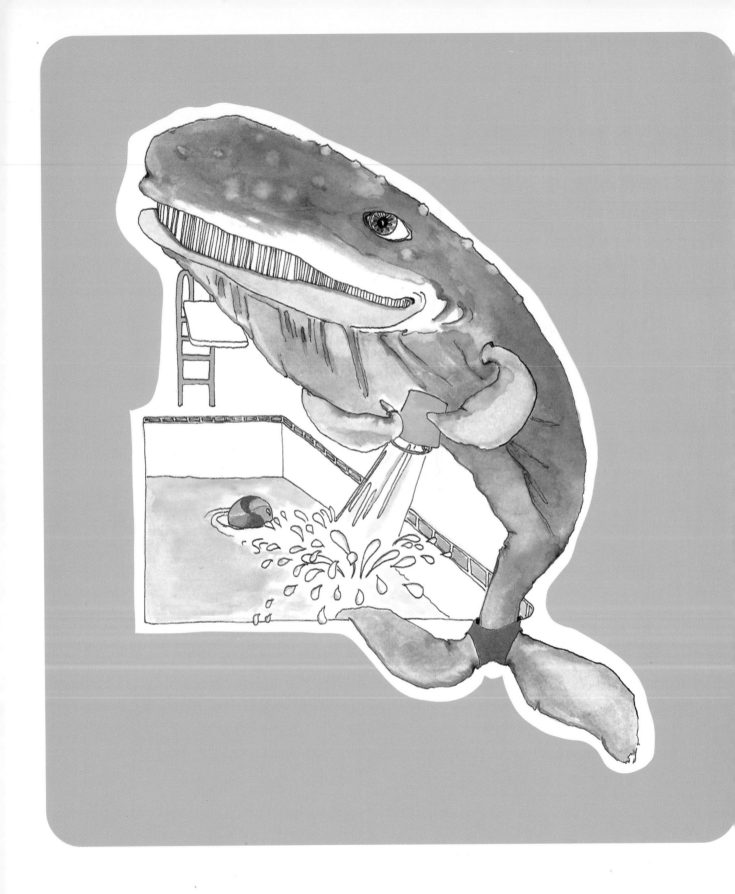

See you with a pail, Whale.

See you at the mine, Porcupine.

See you on a truck, Duck.